For Nettie – S.K.

For Ava, exactly as you are – A.G.

Bloomsbury Publishing, London, Oxford, New York, New Delhi and Sydney

First published in Great Britain in 2018 by Bloomsbury Publishing Plc
50 Bedford Square, London WC1B 3DP

www.bloomsbury.com

BLOOMSBURY is a registered trademark of Bloomsbury Publishing Plc

A CIP catalogue record of this book is available from the British Library

ISBN 978 1 4088 8193 4 (HB)
ISBN 978 1 4088 8194 1 (PB)
ISBN 978 1 4088 8192 7 (eBook)

All papers used by Bloomsbury Publishing are natural, recyclable products made
from wood grown in well managed forests. The manufacturing processes
conform to the environmental regulations of the country of origin

Printed in China by Leo Paper Products, Heshan, Guangdong

1 3 5 7 9 10 8 6 4 2

Being a
PRINCESS
is Very Hard Work

Sarah KilBride

Ada Grey

BLOOMSBURY
LONDON OXFORD NEW YORK NEW DELHI SYDNEY

Being a **princess** is
very hard work,
there's so much to do
it would drive you berserk!

The Royal Academy
for
Perfect
Princesses

Like sitting on thrones . . .

for **hours**
if required,

and smiling and waving even when tired.

A princess, I've heard, has no time to play –
she's **too** busy practising handshakes all day.

She does what she's told with a smile and good grace,

no sticking out tongues or making a face.

No burping or farting
or picking your nose –
a princess should smell
like a beautiful rose.

Don't talk with your mouth **full** . . . please be polite –
it's ever so **tiring** doing it **right**.

Finish your plate and eat **all** your greens,
while keeping a lookout for horrible queens.

Being a princess –
there's no time to rest!
Spinning wheels, dragons . . .
she's put to the test.

Princesses **must** run in a **really** long dress –

at the end of the story,
they're never a mess.

No nits in their hair and
no scabby knees.

They **never** trip over or fall out of trees.

No bouncing allowed on a **big** trampoline –
a princess must **always** stay tidy and clean!

No, being a princess just sounds like a bore.
Being a real girl is better, I'm sure.
We think you are perfect so please don't change . . .
Life with a princess would be rather strange.

We **love** your tangles and socks that fall down.
We **love** your big smile and also your frown.

Your climbing, your falling and **ALL** of your noise.
Your sharing, your squeezing when playing with toys.

We **love** how quickly you make a mess.
You're so much more **fun** than a shiny princess.

We **love** you because you are who you are –
to us you are perfect, a **real superstar!**